Dune Dragons

INDIGORIVER
PUBLISHING

Dune Dragons

Gretchen Rose
with illustrations by: Dianita Ceron

Indigo River Publishing

This book is a work of fiction. Names, characters, locations, and incidents are the product of the author's imagination or are used fictitiously. Any resemblance to actual events or persons, living or dead, is coincidental

Editors: Justyn Newman and Regina Cornell
Cover & Interior Design: mycustombookcover.com
Cover and interior illustrations: Dianita Ceron

Indigo River Publishing
3 West Garden Street, Ste. 352
Pensacola, FL 32502
www.indigoriverpublishing.com

Ordering Information:
Quantity sales: Special discounts are available on quantity purchases by corporations, associations, and others. For details, contact the publisher at the address above.

Orders by US trade bookstores and wholesalers: Please contact the publisher at the address above.

Printed in the United States of America

Library of Congress Control Number: 2019943293
ISBN: 978-1-950906-00-0

First Edition

With Indigo River Publishing, you can always expect great books, strong voices, and meaningful messages. Most importantly, you'll always find . . . words worth reading.

Dedicated with the greatest respect to the National Parks Service, whose employees remain as vigilant as Mother Bear, in the safekeeping of this breathtakingly beautiful, national treasure, the Sleeping Bear Dunes.

Table of Contents

Prologue

The boy sat on the old man's lap. "Tell us the Legend of the Sleeping Bear, Grandpa."

"Yes." The little girl's head rested upon her grandfather's chest. "The Sleeping Bear," she lisped.

The old man chuckled. "I've told it to you many times. Why do you want to hear such a sad story?"

"Please." The children snuggled closer to their grandfather. "Tell us."

"All right," Grandfather said. "Then off to bed with you."

THE LEGEND OF THE SLEEPING BEAR

Long ago, in a time of great famine, Mother Bear and her two starving cubs found themselves on the Wisconsin shore. Vainly, they searched for food, anything to fill their empty bellies. But the earth was barren. Wistfully, they gazed across the vast, watery expanse toward Michigan, the land of plenty. Finally, driven by hunger, the three launched themselves out in an attempt to swim to the other side. As they set off for the Michigan coast, Mother Bear urged her cubs on. They swam a great distance, were only twelve miles from shore, when one of the babies sank beneath the surface and drowned. Frantically, Mother Bear offered up words of encouragement to her remaining cub. But, weak from hunger and exhaustion, he, too, perished.

Eventually, Mother Bear reached the Michigan coast. Wearily, she dragged herself to a place not far from the shoreline and collapsed. Grief-stricken, she looked out over the Great Lake that had claimed her dear ones. As she gazed across the shimmering blue water, two splendid landmasses slowly rose up and broke the surface. The Earth Mother, the Great Spirit Manitou, had chosen to mark the graves of Mother Bear's cubs with a pair of beautiful islands still visible today: North and South Manitou Islands. These islands mark the spots where the cubs disappeared. And the Sleeping Bear Dune pays homage to the vigilant mother bear who, to this day, continues to watch over her cubs.

"And that is the Legend of the Sleeping Bear," Grandfather said, making as if to rise from his chair, but the children wrapped their arms about him and pleaded for another story.

“One more, Grandpa.” The boy patted the man’s whiskered cheek.

“Please, Grandfather,” the little girl said, plugging a thumb in her mouth.

The old man hesitated. Another tale came to mind—one his grandparents had recounted to him when he was a boy. “One more story,” he said, settling back into his chair. “But then to bed!”

Chapter 1

The Legend

"There is another legend about these parts," Grandpa said. "And it's a happier tale."

"What?" the small girl asked.

"It's the Legend of the Dune Dragons, my dear."

"Dragons?" The boy's eyes lit up. "There were dragons here?"

"Oh yes! The most amazing creatures that ever roamed the earth."

"What did they look like, Grandpa?" The girl replanted the thumb in her mouth and nestled into the crook of her grandfather's arm.

"Sweetheart, they were magical creatures. Beautiful, with their mirror-like scales and their black-rimmed golden eyes! And, despite their ability to spew fire while breathing, they were a gentle lot. In fact, the Dune Dragons came to these parts to escape violence.

"For generations they'd lived in harmony with man. Dragon flesh tastes something like lizard, not at all tasty! So the Dras were not hunted but left in peace. Unfortunately, that all ended when tribe rose up against clan, and blood spilled over the land. Humans thought to harness the dragons' ability to fly and spew flames. What an advantage it would give them in their battles! They could fly on the dragons' backs, shoot arrows from the sky, command the Dras to exhale dragon breath, and set fire to their enemy's villages!

"The dragons were horrified at this prospect. Eventually, they decided they had no other choice but to leave that place and find a new home. They embarked on a perilous journey across a vast ocean, winging their way to a new land. Younglings, not strong enough to fly the distance, were strapped to the backs of their parents. Just as Mother Bear and her cubs did, the dragons, too, suffered from hunger. Although the sea teemed with fish, the dragons refused to eat them, for they were plant eaters. Luckily, the dragons found their way to Michigan, a relative wilderness. I say 'luckily' because the Dras loved water."

"And Michigan is home of the Great Lakes!" the boy exclaimed.

"Lots of water," his sister added, her eyelids drooping.

"Yes! The Dune Dragons were delighted with their new home . . ."

***

Chryllis turned to his best friend, Jilly. "Here I go," he said, puffing out his chest.

"Oh, Chryllis, be careful," Jilly said.

"Careful, schmerful." Chryllis pretended to be brave. In fact, the prospect terrified him. Perched at the edge of the dune, he eyed the sheer slope that ended in the Great Lake far below. How could he possibly accomplish such a feat? he wondered. All his life he'd looked forward to this very moment, and now he dithered.

"Come on, Chryllis," an older Dra boy shouted as he tore past and leapt off the precipice. "Take your birthday juuump."

"Yeah, Chryllis," another Dra teen jeered, as he, too, sprang from the cliff. "Don't be an old cooold breath!" The two boys laughed uproariously as they slid down the dune into the sparkling waters.

"You can do it, Chryllis," Jilly encouraged, her gold-flecked eyes gleaming. Chryllis screwed up his courage, determined to impress his fearless friend. "Whee!" he shrieked as he threw himself off the dune. In the next instant, something magical happened: he was dune-sliding! And, just as he'd always imagined, it was thrilling! Slick as mercury, his silvery-scaled back zinged down the steep incline effortlessly.

"Watch out!" Jilly screamed as Chryllis nearly collided with a large rock outcropping. But her words were lost on the boy Dra. The world was rushing toward him at breakneck speed. Such excitement! In the next moment, his exhilaration turned to bewilderment.

"Oww!" Chryllis howled as he became entangled in the branches of a fallen tree. The abrupt halt to his descent caused his head to snap back and strike a rock. Dazed, Chryllis saw stars.

Watching from her vantage point atop the dune, Jilly didn't know what to think. Chryllis was an unmoving speck far beneath her. Perhaps he was merely playing a joke, she reasoned. He would do anything to make her laugh. But when time dragged and Chryllis still hadn't moved, Jilly figured he was in trouble.

"Help!" she screeched, but the wind and the crashing of the waves beating against the shoreline swallowed her cries. What could she do? Jilly wondered. Dras were not allowed to dune-slide until the age of ten, and younglings were expressly forbidden to test their wings until their teens. Dare she break the rules? "Desperate times call for desperate measures," she muttered, wisps of smoke curling from her flared nostrils. "I'm coming," Jilly cried as she hurled herself off the dune.

Jilly had thought to dune-slide. But, without giving it a thought, she raised her wings and let them carry her down. "Oh!" Jilly exclaimed when she realized what she'd done. Flying on one's own power was delightful! But she couldn't think about that now; she had to remain focused on Chryllis. He hadn't budged. She needed to cross the distance between them, and the sooner the better!

In the next instant, Jilly splayed her long-nailed toes into the steep incline. "I'm here, Chryllis," she breathed, and a tiny flame escaped her lips.

Through half-opened eyes, Chryllis detected a flicker of light. "More stars," he muttered at the sight of Jilly's fire breath.

Jilly's concern for her friend morphed to all-out panic. She'd broken Dra law to save Chryllis. He needed to cooperate and quickly. Otherwise, they'd surely be discovered and punished! Jilly clapped her hands in front of her friend's snout. "Wake up, Chryllis!" she urged.

Chryllis struggled to regain his senses, but the blow to his head had made him groggy and slow. When the world finally came into focus, Jilly's lovely face appeared before him. "Jilly," he gushed. "You're so pretty!"

"Not now, Chryllis," Jilly cried, frantically attempting to disentangle her friend from the dead tree's clutches. "We need to get out of here!"

Before either of them knew it, Jilly had successfully extricated him. In the next instant, the young dragon was rocketing down the steep slope. Dune-sliding was such fun that Chryllis forgot all about the bump on his head. He called out to his friend. "Come on, Jilly! Dune-slide with me."

Jilly shook her head in annoyance. At times, Chryllis could be very exasperating! But then she reconsidered. Why not? she wondered. They were probably already in trouble. They might as well have fun before paying the consequences. Throwing caution to the wind, Jilly pushed off. And then she, too, was zipping down the dune with lightning-fast speed.

When Chryllis plunged into the icy cold water, Jilly was right behind him. "Awesome!" Chryllis exclaimed, as Jilly's head broke the surface. And then the two were laughing and frolicking in the lake, while overhead the Dra teens soared on warm air currents rising above the much cooler body of water.

***

Chryllis hurried toward his cave. In all the excitement, he'd nearly forgotten the Council Gathering tonight. But when, as if by magic, a large black crow suddenly appeared before him, he stopped in his tracks.

"Saw you dune-sliding, kid," the crow said. "Too bad about your getting wrapped up in that uprooted sapling. But, all in all, a decent first run, you ask me."

"Hi, Cole! What's up?" Chryllis asked.

"Same old, same old. The cherries are ripe. Me and the boys been having cherry-pit-spitting contests. And the winner would be—"

"Let me guess," Chryllis interrupted. He poked the big, black bird playfully. "Yours truly!"

"Bingo!"

"Maybe I'll join you in the orchard tomorrow," Chryllis said. "There's nothing I like more than cherries."

"Um-hum. Mighty fine!"

"Well, I've got to be getting home now. See you tomorrow, Cole."

Cole winked an enormous yellow eye. "You're on," he said. "Tomorrow, kid."

Chapter 2

Unwelcome Neighbors

"Chryllis, where have you been?" Elya eyed her sandy, wet youngling. But she was in a hurry and eager to be on her way. "Never mind," she said. "Your father's already left, and we need to join him at the meadow, pronto!"

Chryllis breathed a sigh of relief. Once more he'd managed to escape punishment for having broken the rules. Little did he know that his minor infraction would pale in comparison to an event that was to rock the entire Dra colony.

Chryllis hated having to be strapped to Elya's back to make the journey. Hadn't Jilly lifted her wings and flown today? he brooded. Surely he could do the same, he thought. But then he glanced down at the undulating hills of green and gold, and his black mood lifted.

"Saw you on the dune today, Chryllis," a Dra teen shouted. He winged past, showing off with a muscular body roll. "Way-ho!" he cried, pumping a forearm in the air.

"Way-ho!" Chryllis said, eyeing the older boy and wishing he could be beating his way to the gathering on his own power. But then the youth turned back, rewarding him with a thumbs-up, and Chryllis thought maybe he hadn't made a complete mess of things today.

"Way-ho, Chryllis!" Jilly's sweet voice came to him like a familiar melody. In the next moment she was beside him, perched astride Leezla's back.

"Way-ho, Jilly," Chryllis said. "Evening, Miss Leezla-Dra."

"Chryllis, I hear you made your dune-sliding debut today," the large female exclaimed.

Elya craned her neck and glared at Chryllis. "You did?" she asked.

"Yes, Ma-Dra," Chryllis said. "I'm ten, you know."

"Well, that explains a few things," Elya muttered under her breath. And then she turned back to her friend. "Hello, Leezla."

"Oh, Miss Elya-Dra," Jilly gushed, "you would have been so proud. Chryllis is a natural dune-slider. Took to it like a fish to water."

"Humph!" Elya snorted, angling her wings and nosing down toward the earth.

"We'll see about that!"

Cheered by Jilly's words, Chryllis told himself it didn't matter if he couldn't fly on his own just yet. Before long he'd be soaring out over the dunes with the best of them! It was great fun to be out late, he thought, and not just a baby Dra. He was ten, after all, and fast becoming aware of the importance of such gatherings. He needed to start paying attention, he decided, and figure out what really happened at these events rather than just spending the time tearing after Jilly.

Following closely on Elya's tail, Leezla swooped toward the open space below. Surrounded by a thick copse of enormous trees, the clearing was impossible to miss. In the moment before they sailed down into the meadow, Chryllis caught Jilly's eye and the two smiled at one another. And then they were whizzing toward the earth at a heart-pounding speed!

The elders were clustered around the ceremonial fire in order of their rank. There was no discrimination between the sexes in the Dra colony, for females were considered equal to their male counterparts. Elya and Leezla unstrapped their younglings without a backward glance and hastened to their places next to their mates, two rows removed from the inner circle.

Chryllis tumbled backward down his mother's tail. He somersaulted onto the ground and didn't stop until his head struck a rock. Stunned, he could do nothing but blink his eyes. More careful in her dismount, Jilly slid down Leezla's back and landed, with a plop, in a sitting position. She leapt to her feet and rushed to her friend's side. "Chrylly," she cried, "get up!"

"Argh," Chryllis moaned, rubbing the lump on his head. "What . . . ?"

"Never mind, silly!" Jilly said, planting a kiss on Chryllis's silvery noggin. "You're fine. Let's go!"

***

A group of younglings had gathered on a small rise to one side of the clearing. Jilly and Chryllis had no trouble finding them, for the glow from a blazing campfire shone like a beacon in the gathering darkness. The Dra children were giddy for having been allowed to stay out past their bedtimes, and the high-pitched ring of their laughter echoed off the dunes to the west.

The two latecomers hurried toward the younglings and teens who were playing in the field. "I've brought corn!" one of the older boys cried just as Jilly and Chryllis joined the throng.

"Me too," another said, clutching several dry-husked ears in his hands.

"Pop it," the young Dras demanded.

And then the group took up the chant: "Pop it! Pop it!"

Needing no more encouragement, the boys began tossing ears of corn high into the air. Before a cob could fall to the ground, one youngster or another would aim his or her dragon breath in its direction. The exhaled licks of flame transformed the kernels into fat white puffs that popped off the cob and swirled about. Soon, a flurry of fluffy white popcorn was snowing down upon them. The young Dras were delighted at the spectacle. They careened about, eyes to the sky, while attempting to catch the puffs in open mouths. In no time, Dras were crashing into one another or tripping over their own long-nailed toes.

Chryllis smacked into Jilly, and they both toppled to the ground. "Oh, Jilly," Chryllis cried, spitting out an un-popped kernel, "sorry!"

Jilly scooped up a handful of popped corn and threw it at Chryllis. "What fun!" she exclaimed.

***

Elya cast her eyes about the assembly. Their comments were growing more heated by the moment, and her apprehension ticked up accordingly. Man was coming, and that meant one thing only: trouble!

"We must leave!" a voice from the crowd thundered.

"Yes," another shouted. "Now!"

Elya remembered a time when the Dras had coexisted with humans. For many years the two species had lived side by side in harmony. It wasn't until one clan decided that a neighboring tribe was its enemy that trouble began. Perhaps the language difference contributed to the mounting distrust, or maybe it had to do with the rights to new hunting grounds. Whatever the reason, they sought to destroy one another. And that is when the Dras were pressed into an unwilling service.

"Breathe fire," a surly, heavy-browed human commanded. Restrained in a confining harness, the Dra huffed and puffed, but to no avail; despite his best efforts, he found himself incapable of exhaling flames.

"I cannot," the Dra said. "It just doesn't happen unless I mean it to."

The man lashed the Dra with a rawhide whip. "Then mean it," he commanded.

Elya shuddered at the painful memory. Perhaps it would be best to leave this place and find another, she thought, one unspoiled by humans.

***

A loud trumpeting rent the air, and the young Dras stopped their romping. "We need to go, Jilly!" Chryllis said, mindful of the summons.

Jilly and Chryllis approached the Elders' Circle expecting to find the Dras bidding cheery farewells to neighbors and friends. Instead, they came upon a scene of turmoil and unrest.

"We must arm ourselves and prepare for battle," a strident voice cried out.

"Arm ourselves?" Leezla cried. "With what? Dragon fire?"

"Dras don't bear arms," Elya said. "We are a peaceful lot. We don't have stomachs for conflict."

"We must leave this place!" an agitated Dra shouted.

Kahn, a white-whiskered elder, raised his forearms, palms toward the crowd. "It has been decided," he said. "We will stay through the winter, keeping to our caves and as far from the humans as possible. In the spring—after our long sleep—we will revisit the matter. Who knows what may occur over the passage of time? Perhaps we will awaken to find that the humans have moved to another place."

Chapter 3

Wait and See

Back in their cave, Elya and Ulf explained the recent events to their sleepy-eyed son. "I don't know how to convey to you the horror of man's wars," Elya said. "Humans battle one another, whereas we Dras venerate peace and harmony."

"But, mom—" Chryllis protested halfheartedly.

"No buts, Chryllis!" Ulf cut him off. "Listen to me, son." The towering dragon drew the boy's face toward his. "Man wants only to exploit us."

***

Far away, upon what is known today as the Wisconsin shore, a dispirited band of humans had gathered. They were a sorry lot, weary from their trek, and desiring nothing more than food and comfort. Just as Mother Bear had done so long ago, these people—hungry and displaced—cast yearning eyes across the great body of water to what we now call Michigan. Cronyn, their leader, pointed toward the east. "Tomorrow we begin the journey," he said.

The humans endured many days of hardship, paddling their boats by day and making camp in the evenings. By the time they were in sight of the magnificent coastline, they were exhausted.

Just as they prepared to come ashore, the sun slipped below the horizon, and the towering Sleeping Bear Dunes reflected it and glowed as if on fire. The people thought this was a good sign. They gazed toward the place they hoped would offer a better life. "This shall be our new home," Cronyn said.

***

"They're coming!" Chryllis bounced up and down with the exuberance of a youngling. In his excitement, he could hardly keep from flying. His untested wings kept rising, and he wanted nothing more than to let them carry him far away over the dunes.

"Yes, they are, and I have a very bad feeling about it, Chryllis," Elya said. "Remember what the elders advised: we are to stay as far away from them as possible, avoid contact."

"But I've never seen a human," Chryllis grumbled. "And what are we to do? Keep to the caves day and night?"

"No! But we are to maintain a safe distance. Whatever you do, do not allow yourself to be lured into their camp. Humans are not to be trusted."

***

The Great Lake stretched before them as far as the eye could see. The people were wary; they knew the journey they were about to embark upon would be a perilous one. The rudimentary crafts they'd fashioned from hollowed-out logs could easily capsize should a storm suddenly brew. Determined, they climbed aboard their canoes and set out across the vast body of water. Huge finned creatures slid silently beneath them as they skimmed across the lake's surface. When, at last, they reached what is now known as the National Lakeshore, Cronyn raised an arm, signaling that their journey had ended. "This place is as good as any," he said. "Let us stop here and make camp."

The humans were industrious and quickly adapted to their new surroundings. Overnight, they created a small settlement comprised of hide-covered structures. In the next weeks, they discovered a land as bounteous as they'd hoped. The lake teemed with trout and whitefish, and the forests were alive with deer, turkey, and rabbit. The humans did not go hungry, and they congratulated themselves for having found this place.

Weeks went by with no contact between the Dras and the new settlers. Occasionally, a human would report the sighting of a fantastical creature with wings and silvery scales. But these accounts were not taken seriously; no one believed such beings existed. As for the Dras, they were well aware of the comings and goings of their new neighbors. But they were careful not to expose themselves, which was not difficult, for it was now time for them to hibernate in their dune caves throughout the long winter months.

While they slept, the human colony flourished.

***

As the first light of dawn spread over the eastern horizon, Elya emerged from her warren at the foot of the dunes. She squinted in the bright sunlight, for the earth wore a crusty white scrim that sparkled like diamonds. Tender shoots of green poked up through patches of white, and tiny green buds were popping out on trees still laden with snow.

Elya resisted the urge to fly over the human settlement to see what progress had been made in the months since she'd last seen it. Instead, she trotted in the other direction, toward a thick stand of trees. Once there, she relaxed, knowing she could not be easily detected. Her family needed food—nuts, dried cherries, tubers—whatever she could find. It had been a particularly long, hard winter, and her store of staples was much depleted.

Elya breathed fire, melting a small patch of snow beneath a walnut tree, and set about gathering what nuts she could find. Thus employed, her sensitive ears detected an unusual sound: human speech. And the speakers were fast approaching!

Terrified, she raised her wings, and a current of air lifted her to a perch high atop a towering pine tree. She'd only just settled onto a sturdy limb when two men traipsed into the space she'd occupied mere moments before. Elya's heart raced. She dared not breathe for fear of making a sound and risking detection. The humans stopped directly beneath her, gazing at the imprints of her long-nailed toes in the patches of snow. They spoke to one another in hushed tones, seemingly pondering the meaning of the strangely shaped depressions.

It was only a matter of minutes—which seemed an eternity to Elya—before the pair continued on. She kept her eyes glued to the rapidly retreating figures. When they had vanished from view, she flew off in the opposite direction, toward her cave.

Chapter 4

The Trap

Chryllis lay curled in his nest, snoring softly. The cave was surprisingly warm under its melting blanket of snow. But a trickle of icy water had managed to seep through the layers of rock and sand that comprised the cave's ceiling, and a droplet collected over the drowsing youngling's head. The bead of water grew larger, swelling until it finally separated from the roof of the cave and landed with a splat on the Dra boy's head.

"Wha . . . ?" Chryllis awoke with a start. "Mmph!" In the next moment he leapt up and trotted to his parents' nest only to find it empty. They'd probably left the cave in search of breakfast, he thought. Whereas grown Dras periodically awoke during their hibernation in order to forage for food, it had been months since he'd been outside. Suddenly, the close quarters felt confining rather than cozy, and Chryllis had an irresistible urge to venture outside; he could hardly wait to meet up with Jilly to see how she'd fared the long winter's confinement.

Chryllis bounded out from the dark cave into a sunshiny world. Although he was eager to reconnect with his friend, he found that his knees were wobbly from long months of disuse. Quickly regaining his balance, he gazed about at a world transforming before his very eyes. There was a steady drip-drip-dripping as icy sheaths encasing trees and undergrowth melted away. Blades of grass were springing up everywhere, seeking the sun's warmth.

"Chryllis!" a familiar voice called. The young Dra whirled around to find Jilly beaming at him. "Hello, old sleepyhead," she teased. "Thought you'd never wake up!"

"I'm awake now," Chryllis said. "When did you get up?"

"Days ago!" Jilly grabbed his forearm. "Come on. I've got something to show you."

Chryllis and Jilly gazed out over the frozen expanse to the west. The beach was covered in a crust of rapidly melting snow laced with sand, and the vast sheet of ice shrouding the enormous lake was beginning to break up. Huge blocks of it had been carried ashore on underlying currents and were now piled one atop another in what had become a dazzling wall of ice. "Wow," Chryllis exclaimed, "it's magical!"

"I know," Jilly said. "We can pretend it's our ice castle."

The two younglings chased one another around the shimmering tower, sliding down its slick sides, occasionally flapping their wings just enough to cause them to sail inches above the icy surfaces. They didn't dare actually fly. But, having newly emerged from their months of hibernation, they doubted the elders would fault them for this small transgression. Soon, they become so absorbed in their game that they failed to feel the eyes of men upon them.

Concealed in a thicket of trees, Cronyn and his brother Thor gazed at the two Dras in wonderment. The humans were protected from the cold by garments made of tanned hides, and their feet were clad in fur-lined boots. Rather than speak and risk detection, they nodded and gestured to one another in silent communication.

"Whee!" Chryllis cried, tearing around the icy ridge in pursuit of Jilly. But his cry of delight became a strangled gasp as he came face to face with one of the scariest beasts he'd ever encountered. Chryllis pivoted, doing an about-face, only to find another human directly in front of him, this one wielding a length of rope. The young Dra ducked and slid away, but Jilly was not so fortunate. Unsuspecting, she rounded the wall of ice only to be similarly confronted. "Run, Jilly!" Chryllis commanded. The girl Dra didn't hesitate; she tore off across the melting sheet of ice and headed out over the bay.

Cronyn and Thor turned toward Chryllis. As one, they moved toward him. The youngling retreated until he found himself backed against an unyielding, frozen wall with no possible means of escape. And that's when one of the men began twirling a length of rope. Mesmerized, Chryllis could only stare helplessly as the loop rose up—seemingly in slow motion—up, up, above him.

"Chryllis," Jilly cried, "look out!" But it was no use. The noose hovered over him, as if in defiance of gravity. But then the lariat plummeted, coming to rest on his long neck. Jilly watched in horror as her friend was lassoed. But then her own predicament demanded her full attention; the ice floe she was standing on was sprouting an enormous fissure. "Help!" Jilly screamed, as the block of ice tipped and swayed. There was nothing else to do but fly, and, having set her mind to it, she flapped her wings and rose skyward. Jilly sailed toward Chryllis, who was thrashing about in an effort to free himself. But he was no match for the two powerfully built men. They held tightly to the rope's end, determined to make the Dra their captive. Jilly dove down and thrust out a forearm. "Take my hand," she cried. At the same time, she lashed out at the men with her spiked tail.

Cronyn and Thor backed away as Chryllis reached for Jilly's outstretched limb. "Fly," Jilly commanded once his hand was clasped in hers.

Chryllis did as he was told; he spread his wings, and before he knew it his feet had left the ground and he was flying beside Jilly!

"Here we go!" Jilly exclaimed. The younglings soared over the treetops, the two men dangling beneath them, taking the ride of their lives. Of course, the men couldn't have hung on forever, but Jilly soon tired of this enterprise. "Breathe fire," she said, nodding toward the length of rope below them.

Almost immediately, Chryllis realized what Jilly was up to. He exhaled a fiery blast, and Jilly did the same. Their aim was true, and a section of the rope quickly burned until it was completely severed. No longer tethered, the men plummeted toward the earth. Fortunately for them, they had a soft landing in a blanket of snow.

Free of the men, Jilly and Chryllis flew above the treetops, thrilled by the exhilarating experience of flying on their own power. They swooped and soared, alternately holding hands and pushing off from one another. But, in a matter of minutes, the two were struck by the enormity of their brush with danger. They'd barely escaped capture! This was not a time for merriment. Chryllis and Jilly's spirits evaporated with each downward whoosh of their wings, so that by the time they planted their spiked toes into the sodden ground, they felt utterly dispirited.

Jilly sighed. "I guess we'd better go home," she said, reaching up to unfasten the noose that hung loosely about her friend's neck.

Chryllis agreed. "We'll have to tell what happened."

Jilly scowled. "I know. Let's hope we don't get into too much trouble."

***

"Chryllis!" The sleek, black bird swooped down from the sky and landed on the Dra boy's shoulder.

"Oh hi, Cole," Chryllis said.

"Hi yourself, kid," the crow replied. "How's tricks?"

"Uhh—"

"Might as well fess up. Me and the boys saw you and that girl of yours flying out over the lake."

"But . . . it's like this . . . ," Chryllis stammered.

"Not to worry." The crow winked a gleaming eye. "We can keep our beaks shut. You're in enough hot water as it is."

Dejected, Chryllis hung his head. "I suppose I am."

"Ah, it'll be okay. You had to, right?"

"Well yeah, for sure! Those . . . *beasts* tried to capture me. Who knows what they would have done?"

"Bad business, humans." The crow shook his head in disgust.

"So what's up with you, Cole? Any news?" Chryllis asked, eager to change the subject.

"Same old, same old. Cherry blossoms are popping out. Real pretty. Won't be long till we'll be having cherry-pit-spitting contests."

"I do love cherries!"

"You and me both, kid." Suddenly Cole's attention was diverted; he'd spied a fat worm poking his head up out of a tiny hole in the ground. With a flap of wings, the crow rose up from Chryllis's shoulder. "But for now, it's the early bird that gets the worm," he cried as he flew off.

"Yuck. I'd rather eat dirt," Chryllis muttered.

Chapter 5

Captured

The ceremonial fire burned brightly, illuminating faces that wore dark expressions. Tonight, the younglings had not been allowed to go off by themselves and play. Instead, they'd been instructed to stay close to their mothers' sides and to remain silent unless told to do otherwise. There was a sense of urgency in the air, and the Dras refrained from their usual easy banter, for tonight's topic of discussion was of the gravest importance: the preservation of the colony.

At the circle's core, a group of elders spoke in low voices, while the last stragglers hurried to take whatever place in the gathering their rank determined. When all were settled, Kahn rose to his full height. "It has come to pass as we feared it might," he began. Despite his many years, the venerable elder's voice resounded throughout the clearing. "Man has made a move against us. The reason for tonight's meeting is to decide what course of action should be taken to maintain the safety and integrity of our colony."

"I heard they tried to kidnap one of our younglings," a voice from the crowd interrupted.

"Yes, that's what I was told," another Dra said.

"Order!" Kahn raised his arms to silence those who would speak out of turn. "You are not misinformed. The Council and I have questioned the younglings involved in this incident." He gestured toward Chryllis and Jilly, who were seated beside Elya and Ulf and Leezla. "They are lucky to be alive and with us this evening." Chryllis and Jilly exchanged wide-eyed looks as they recalled their most recent human encounter. "The Dras are a peace-loving race. We will not be drawn into war. But neither will we allow our younglings to be captured and exploited."

"I should say not," an angry voice from the crowd interjected.

Kahn favored that Dra with a stern look. "We shall overlook this latest transgression," he said. "We will keep our distance, tilt our scales, and present our reflective shields when in the presence of man. Mother Dras shall teach their children the ancient art of becoming invisible. But, in the event of another such incident, we will be forced to leave and find a new home—somewhere untainted by humans."

***

Time passed with only a few man-sightings. On those instances, the Dras tilted their mica-like scales, making themselves invisible to the human eye. Thankfully, there'd been no more mention of leaving, for summer was the most delightful time of year in the Great Lakes region.

Younglings hooted and hollered as they leapt off the dunes, sliding down on their backs into the shimmering waters below, while overhead the Dra teens swooped and soared on updrafts. But Chryllis and Jilly were not among them. They'd been charged with tending to Leezla's young niece, Baabaazuzu.

"My sister needs a rest," Leezla said. "Glenis is plumb worn out from caring for that little one."

"Aw, Ma," Jilly protested, "Chryllis and I were going to meet out on the dunes. It's a perfect day for sliding."

"You heard me, young lady," Leezla said. "Baabaazuzu's too young to be near the water. You and Chryllis can take her to the cherry orchard. And don't come back until dinnertime." Leezla made a shooing motion with her hand. "Go on now!"

"Yes, ma'am," Jilly said, as she hastened in the direction of her aunt's dune cave.

***

The fairy-white blossoms of the cherry trees had long since been replaced by lush green leaves and ripening fruit, and in the neighboring fields spiky cornstalks had nearly grown to full height. Chryllis lay recumbent in the tall grass, gazing at the wispy clouds overhead. Jilly stood beside him, and baby Zuzu sat at her feet with her chubby legs sprawled. "Look, Zuzu." Jilly reached up and snapped off a tiny cherry. "What's this?" she asked.

Zuzu gazed up at Jilly, her gold-flecked eyes enormous in her chubby face. "Di!" Zuzu said.

"No, no, silly! *Cher*-ry," Jilly corrected.

"Chree," Zuzu replied.

"*Cher*-ry," Jilly repeated. "Here, try it." She popped the unripe cherry in Zuzu's mouth.

"Poot!" Zuzu grimaced and promptly spit out the tart fruit. "No like chree."

With a flurry of feathers, Cole tumbled out of the sky and landed next to Chryllis. "The kid's not bad," the blackbird said, while brushing himself off and regaining his composure. "In another month, she'll be spitting cherry pits with the best of us."

"Chree," Zuzu said, studying the stout crow.

"Yeah, whatever," Cole replied.

"Hi, Cole," Chryllis said. "This is baby Zuzu, and you've met Jilly."

"Hello, Cole," Jilly said.

"How do?" Cole replied. "Nice day, huh? Say, have you seen Madge or Toofus?"

"No, why?" Chryllis sat up, eyeing Cole curiously.

"Me and the boys were supposed to meet them here," Cole said. But his words were drowned out by a raucous cacophony as daylight fled. Cole and the Dras looked skyward only to witness thousands of chattering passenger pigeons winging overhead. It was as though someone had thrown a dark blanket over the sun.

"Chree," Zuzu cried.

"Birds," Jilly said. "Lots and lots of birds." And then the pigeons were gone, and the sun showed its bright face again.

"Yeah, those guys travel en masse!" Cole agreed. "Me, I prefer small groups." As if on cue, four black birds appeared in the cherry tree above them. "There are my boys," he said. The crows greeted the Dras with nods and a flutter of iridescent black wings.

"Hello, felloths." A whiskered creature lumbered toward them. "Long time no sthee," he lisped through his prominent front teeth.

"Hey there, Toofus," Chryllis said. "What've you been up to?"

The beaver raised his powerful tail. "Practisching," he said.

At that moment, a compact ball of fur trotted toward the small group. "Well, let's hope so," the badger said. "It won't be long before the Summer Games begin. We need to be in tip-top form if we're going to win the Golden Apple."

"You can say that again, Madge," Cole agreed.

Zuzu's eyes grew round while witnessing this exchange. Jilly bent down and took the baby Dra in her arms. "Badger," she said, pointing in Madge's direction. "And that's a beaver." She nodded toward Toofus.

"Babber," Zuzu said.

Toofus and Madge chuckled.

"Cute kid," Cole said. "Let's get to it!"

With that, the crows dove down in aerial formation, their ebony wings beating in unison. They landed beneath a line of fir trees bordering the orchard and quickly scattered in every direction. Sifting through the bed of pine needles, they began collecting pinecones and acorns.

"Do we have time to watch them play?" Chryllis asked Jilly.

"We can stay a while," Jilly replied. "Come on, Zuzu."

The younglings sat on the edge of the clearing, directly behind a recently constructed pyramid comprised of acorns and pinecones, while Zuzu crawled about in the grass, searching for anything she might put in her mouth.

Toofus took his position and began warming up, wagging his tail from side to side, and Cole came to stand directly behind him. At the same time, Madge made her way to the opposite end of the clearing, and the other crows filled out the playing field. Once everyone was properly positioned, Cole cawed loudly, signaling that the practice was to begin.

Never taking her eyes off the beaver, Madge reached down and palmed a large pinecone from atop the pile. She hefted it, shaking her head from side to side, seemingly in no hurry. "She's a cool one," Cole muttered, eyeing Madge approvingly. Toofus raised his tail in anticipation of the badger's next move. Then Madge lobbed the pinecone in Toofus's direction. It lofted through the air toward its mark. The beaver was ready; he smacked the projectile with his powerful tail, and it wafted out over the clearing.

"I cawed it, I cawed it!" a crow in left field cried, catching the pinecone in his beak.

***

"It's baseball!" the boy exclaimed. "They're playing baseball, Gramps."

"Something like," the old man said, nodding his head in agreement. "Long ago the animals lived peacefully with one another. They enjoyed getting together to play games, much as we do."

The baby girl unplugged the thumb from her mouth long enough to remark, "I like baby Zuzu."

"Of course you do, honey," Grandpa replied. "Why, she's nearly the same age as you."

***

Jilly and Chryllis traipsed through the forest, making their way back home to the colony. Exhausted after her exciting day with the younglings, Zuzu traveled piggyback fashion, her forearms wrapped around the boy Dra's neck.

"That wasn't so bad after all," Chryllis said.

"It was fun!" Jilly agreed. "Maybe we could learn to play that game."

"Sure thing! I'll talk to Cole about it."

Unbeknown to the younglings, two humans were watching their every move. Concealed by a canopy of trees, Cronyn and Thor gazed at the Dras in amazement. They'd been given a second opportunity to catch a dragon, and they were determined this attempt would meet with success!

It wasn't until a whoosh of air stirred above them that Chryllis and Jilly looked up and realized their plight. "Look out!" Chryllis cried. Once again, the lasso was wobbling over his head, and it seemed that history was to repeat itself. But the forest was thick with trees, and the descending noose became snagged on a limb.

At that very moment, a ferocious-looking wolverine emerged from the dense tangle of underbrush. With fangs bared, he put himself between the huntsmen and the Dras, snarling at the humans.

Chryllis and Jilly exchanged looks of astonishment. They could hardly believe their eyes. This fearsome creature had appeared out of nowhere to defend them! But then one of the men charged. Cudgel raised, he delivered the wolverine a glancing blow. The wolverine howled in pain and loped off, leaving the Dras defenseless once more.

Coming to their senses, Chryllis and Jilly tilted their scales as they'd been taught and promptly disappeared from view. But baby Zuzu, too young to have mastered that technique, remained visible.

Cronyn and Thor advanced, clubs in hand. They were nearly upon the Dras when Jilly cried out, "Fly, Chryllis!" With a mighty beating of wings, the younglings rose into the air. "Hold tight, Zuzu," Chryllis cautioned, as he felt the baby's arms loosen about his neck. He reached up in an effort to get a firm hold on her, but she was slipping from his grasp!

Zuzu had awakened to mayhem. One moment she'd been drowsing contentedly, and the next she found herself aloft! She cried out in terror, for she'd never flown without being securely strapped to her mother's body.

Chryllis could feel Zuzu sliding down his back. "No!" he howled, his arms flailing as he attempted to catch her. But it was no use.

"Zuzu!" Jilly cried as the baby Dra plunged toward earth and the humans waiting below. Still invisible, Chryllis and Jilly watched in horror as Zuzu landed in a pair of outstretched arms.

Chapter 6

The Plan

Wearing stricken expressions, Chryllis and Jilly cowered in the center of the Elder Council circle. The younglings knew there was nothing they could have done to prevent baby Zuzu's capture. Still, they felt as though this tragedy were somehow their fault.

"Where was it that you encountered the humans?" Kahn asked.

"In the forest between the cherry orchard and the colony," Chryllis said.

The Dra elders exchanged knowing looks. "Younglings shall be expressly forbidden to travel there alone again," Kahn stated. "Are we in agreement?" The others nodded their approval.

"And how was baby Zuzu captured?" another elder asked.

"Oh, it was awful," Jilly replied. "The humans sneaked up on us. As soon as we realized what was happening, Chryllis and

I tilted our scales and disappeared. But Zuzu didn't know how to do that, and she remained visible."

"So, they come for our children," Khan muttered.

"And then, when we decided to fly away," Jilly continued, "Zuzu slipped down Chryllis's back and—"

"I tried to catch her," Chryllis interjected. "I did!"

"It's all right, son," an ancient female Dra said. "You did all you could."

"We find ourselves in a difficult situation," Khan said. "Our safety is jeopardized; the humans intend us harm."

"They have my baby," Glenis wailed. "My sweet girl!"

***

Under cover of darkness, the woodland animals had crept up close to the dragon gathering to listen and observe.

"Well, darn it, we need to do something," Cole said with a flutter of wings. "This is the cherry pits!"

"Sheesh, I guesh so," Toofus agreed, lisping through his protruding front teeth.

"The Dras are actually thinking about leaving," Madge said. "That's horrible!"

"We have to fight," Gryr, the fearsome wolverine, growled. "Take no prisoners!"

"Good thought, Gryr," Madge said. "We need to decide a course of action."

"Grrrr . . . ," Gryr grumbled. "These humans test my patience. I want to . . ." The wolverine quivered with suppressed rage. "Argh! I say we fight!"

"I know," Madge soothed. "They make me crazy too. But we need a plan."

"Whoo-hoo! A plan, a plan!" Hooey dove in to join the animal conference. "Whoo-ya! We must devise a plan!" With a ruffle of wings, the owl landed on the limb of a towering maple tree.

"What do you have you in mind, Hooey?" Madge asked.

"Whoo-emm . . . let me think on it," Hooey said, slowly closing his hooded eyelids.

Seconds ticked by, and the other animals grew restive. They exchanged brief looks and cast furtive glances at the inanimate owl. Finally, Gryr broke the silence. "Dang," he grumbled. "We don't have all night. Get on with it!"

"Hush! These things cannot be hurried," Madge said. But even the patient badger was at her wit's end. A few more moments passed, and Cole could take the suspense no longer. He spread his wings, rose up, and landed next to the owl. "Hooey! Wake cawp!" Cole squawked.

"Wha. . . ?" The owl opened his eyes wide, seemingly confused as to why he'd become the center of attention. But he quickly regained his poise. "Humph! It's elementary, I say . . ."

"Aaannd that means . . . ?" Gryr growled.

"It meansth we need to do somethingth," Toofus interjected.

"Ahem," the owl cleared his throat, and all eyes turned to him. "Of course, we need to assist the Dras and help them rescue baby Zuzu, but we must do so without violence. We will mount a siege, but this battle will be one of wits rather than might. There will be no casualties."

"That's a tall order," Gryr muttered.

"Yes, but Hooey's got it right," Madge said. "This operation will require careful planning."

"Well, letsh get to work then!" Toofus said.

Cole had been deep in thought during this last exchange, but in the next instant, he became animated and rejoined the conversation. "The way I see it," he said, "we take the humans by surprise, snatch the baby Dra at dawn."

"Yes!" Hooey agreed. "We'll send in the field mice before the sun rises. They can wreak all kinds of havoc under the cover of darkness, put the humans at an immediate disadvantage before they've even had time to rub the sleep from their eyes!"

"And before they realize it—" Cole said.

"Zuzu will be in our hands," Hooey interrupted.

"But they're not gonna let her go without putting up a fight!" Gryr muttered.

"And that's where it gets dicey, my friends," Cole said. "Ahh"—he rubbed the tips of his wings together—"this is gonna be a madcap caper!"

***

Chryllis and Jilly lolled just beyond their warren of caves, as did most of the other younglings. It was a perfect day for dune-sliding and gliding above the Great Lake on currents of air. But the dunes remained strangely empty.

"Shoot!" one of the Dra teens grumbled. "We might as well be under house arrest."

"Yeah!" Another teen breathed a small lick of fire. "And it's all because of those two." He nodded toward Jilly and Chryllis.

"That's not true!" Jilly said. "We didn't do anything. And casting blame will not accomplish anything."

The teens hung their heads despondently. "Sorry, Jilly."

"Me too. It's just so frustrating . . ."

"I feel helpless," Chryllis confided to Jilly. "As if it really were my fault somehow."

Jilly placed a forearm on Chryllis's shoulder. "I know. But it's not. Feeling guilty will not get Zuzu back."

Just then, Cole flew down and landed directly in front of the younglings. "Hiya, kids!" he greeted. Then he spun around and addressed the entire group of Dra youngsters. "Too bad about you guys not being allowed to dune-slide or fly, huh?"

"I'll say," one of the teens agreed. "It's the cherry pits!"

"Tough break," Cole said.

"Yeah," Chryllis agreed.

"Well, buck up!" Cole said. "I got some good news for you. Me and the boys have come up with a strategy, a kind of battle plan. And we're going to need your help to sell it to the elders."

"What?" Jilly's eyes grew wide.

"That's right. We're going to nab Zuzu and show those humans a thing or two in the process."

The younglings and teens immediately perked up, and a buzz of excited conversation swirled among their ranks. "Now you're talking!" one of the Dras exclaimed.

"What can we do?" Jilly asked.

"It's like this . . ." Cole beckoned for the Dra kids to come closer.

***

In the ensuing days, the colony was a beehive of activity. Many meetings were held to address particular phases of the battle plan. Every Dra over the age of five was assigned a task.

"Hup, hup," Leezla barked, and the motley group of younglings assembled before her marched in order. "Now fly," she commanded, and the Dra kids spread their wings and rose from the meadow. "Tilt scales," she demanded, and the young Dras dutifully disappeared. "Now, breath fire," she ordered, and the sky was suddenly aglow with licks of flame, seemingly appearing out of nowhere. "Good," Leezla murmured, arching a black brow. "Very good."

A pugnacious rat paced back and forth before a regiment of field mice, barking instructions. "Hug the earth, and run like the wind," he said. "Slip silently into the humans' living quarters through any passageway you find. Knot the laces of their shoes, gnaw at their cudgels, and pry the arrow heads from their shafts. For although you are the smallest in our ranks, your size gives you the advantage; you have the ability to create havoc and confusion, to determine the outcome of the battle before it even begins."

Chapter 7

The Sting

"Eat!" the human demanded as he thrust a steaming bowl toward Zuzu. The baby Dra cringed, backing into the corner of her cage. The smell of cooked game made her gag, and she turned away, weeping.

"Agh!" the man growled. He latched the cage, shaking his head in frustration. "Silly creature. You'll eat soon enough," he muttered as he strode off.

Unbeknown to him, a small girl had witnessed this exchange. She peeked out from behind a wall at the baby Dra, her eyes round in wonderment. Baby Zuzu cried piteously. She missed her mother and the safety of the colony, and she was hungry and cold.

Cautiously the little girl approached Zuzu's cage. "Shh, don't cry," she said.

"Ha!" Zuzu exclaimed, startled. But the little girl gazed at her with such compassion, Zuzu knew in an instant she had nothing to fear. "Kai," the baby dragon said.

"Don't cry," the girl reiterated, brushing a make-believe tear from her eye.

"Kai," Zuzu repeated, dashing tears from her own eyes.

"Yes!" Then the girl pointed to herself. "I'm Alitta," she said, stabbing her chest with an index finger. "Alitta."

Zuzu pointed to her own chest. "Litta," she said.

"No, no, no!" The girl pointed to Zuzu. "You not Alitta. You . . . ?"

Light dawned in Zuzu's eyes. She touched her breastbone. "Zuzu," she replied.

"Zuzu!" Alitta clapped her hands in delight. "Oh, Zuzu," she said, "I'm going to try to get you out of there."

***

The two Dras strolled through the forest in companionable silence. Elya glanced up at Ulf from beneath her long lashes. He was such a capable Dra, she thought, and so strong! She was proud of her mate.

Ulf was the first to speak. "We've done all we could to prepare for the raid," he said. "Thanks to our animal friends, we're as ready as we'll ever be."

"We've come a long way, but I still can't believe that we're actually going to attempt this thing," Elya said.

"Hooey was brilliant, flying to the human settlement under

cover of darkness, pinpointing Zuzu's exact whereabouts."

"If it weren't for him, we'd be running around like ninnies with no idea where to concentrate our efforts," Elya agreed as she linked arms with Ulf.

***

"Hoo, hoo!" Hooey called, swooping down to eye his troops. The field mice were assembled in haphazard ranks, the lines of which kept moving. They were mice, after all, and by nature, jittery; it was impossible for them to maintain perfect order.

"This is scary," a tiny mouse confessed. "I hope there are no dogs or cats!"

"You'll be fine, son," Hooey soothed. "I've made the run myself, winging it, actually. But I'll lead you past the curs and into the encampment, and from there—"

"We'll do fearsome damage," a vole squeaked. "Gnaw through leggings and laces, pry arrow heads from their shafts—"

"We'll show those humans a thing or two," another piped in.

"Baby Zuzu!" a vole exclaimed. And the ranks took up the cry.

"Zuzu, Zuzu!"

"Hookay, men, let's go!" Hooey lifted his wings and rose from his perch. "Forward!"

The rodents surged ahead, eager to begin their tasks. Hooey flew above them, marking their progress and serving as reconnaissance.

Gryr led his pack toward the human settlement. "We are the last resort, my friends," he said. "These Dras are clueless. They insist on nonviolence. But we'll—"

"It's ridiculous," another wolverine interrupted as they trotted through the forest. "We're born fighters; we could easily accomplish this raid on our own. But now, when our skills are most needed, we're hamstrung!"

"We might as well be bunnies or butterflies," another grumbled.

"Not to worry," Gryr said. "Our talents will not be wasted. Trust me. There will be blood!"

"Grrr!" The wolverines barred their fangs and pushed ahead. "Blooood!"

Madge and Toofus ambled beneath a canopy of cherry trees. "The Dras have collected hundreds of pinecones and acorns," Madge said.

"Yeth, and the rabbitsth and sthquirrelsth have done their part asth well," Toofus said. "We've got lotsh of ammo."

"Let's hope we don't run out before we find and rescue Zuzu," Madge said.

***

Inside the human settlement, Zuzu's captors slept. Except for faintly glowing embers in small hearth fires, the interiors of their dwellings were dark. The rodents had long since retreated, their mission of destruction accomplished. The evidence of their efforts was yet to be realized, but one thing was for certain: the humans would awaken to chaos.

Alitta had slept fitfully. She'd had nightmares about an army of giant rodents who meant to harm her. Finally, she crept from her bed of furs and tiptoed through the crude dwelling and out into a night lit by a zillion stars. The small girl gazed up at the black velvet sky radiant with pinpricks of light. "Ahh," she breathed. "Zuzu needs to be free, to live with her family in peace. Oh, Great Spirit, help me help my friend," she prayed.

***

As the first light of dawn bled over the horizon, thousands of mosquitoes, bumblebees, gnats, and wasps swarmed before the human settlement. Cole toppled from the sky and hovered before the agitated clouds. "Good show," he encouraged. "Right on time!" But then he crooked his neck and smacked a wingtip against it. "Agh! Hey, don't bite me! It's them"—Cole turned and indicated the human camp—"those are the guys you're after. Cawed it?"

His answer was a buzz-saw-like thrumming. The clouds of insects pulsed. Hungry pests eager for a human meal were happy to lend their unique skills to the Dras' offensive. "Okeydokey," Cole said. "Cawmence!" And the teeming insects began their attack.

Chapter 8

Deliverance

Suddenly, voices were raised in alarm. Humans leapt from their beds in panic as a wall of flying insects descended upon them. Those that took the time to dress and arm themselves, all the while flailing at their miniscule attackers, were further confounded to find that their footwear and clothing were in tatters, their weapons destroyed.

Moments after the attack of the bloodthirsty hordes, a wave of humans rushed from their dwellings to escape their tormentors only to be met by a salvo of pinecones and acorns. Toofus and his team of beavers had positioned themselves at strategic intervals with pit crews of badgers, rabbits, and squirrels, their sole mission to keep the beavers' tails loaded with pinecones and nuts.

Well rehearsed, they worked with the efficiency of an assembly line. The beavers thwacked their makeshift ammo toward the humans, and the missiles rained down upon those unfortunates like stinging hail.

Cleverly, the forest animals had left only one means of escape: a pathway leading to the lakeshore. In no time, the humans were pounding down that trail, eager to flee their attackers. They bunched together on the shoreline, milling about uncertainly.

"What should we do, Cronyn?" a woman's voice called out.

"Yes, are we to leave the homes we've only just constructed and start anew?" another asked.

"I'm not leaving," Thor bellowed. "We'll fight!"

***

Meanwhile, Alitta had managed to free Baby Zuzu and spirit her away. Unaware of the ensuing conflict, she was heading through the forest with the baby Dra in tow, hoping somehow, magically, to return Zuzu to the Dra colony. But there was a flaw in Alitta's plan: she had no idea where to find the baby Dra's family. Alitta whispered a prayer to the Great Father as she scurried on, Zuzu's hand in hers. "Please help me help my friend," she breathed.

***

"Jiminy," Chryllis grumbled. "Why is it we're consigned to mopping up? What's to mop up? Who knows what's happening while we sit and wait for the signal?" The two friends were in the last line of the youngling regiment and had been left to their own devices. The other Dra kids had long since broken ranks and were testing their wings or playing games to pass the time.

"I know," Jilly agreed despondently. "It's the cherry pits!"

Chryllis scanned the perimeter and quickly surmised that no one was paying them any attention. He raised a black brow conspiratorially and leaned in toward Jilly. "I have an idea," he said.

"Oh, no!" Jilly exclaimed, shaking her head in mock horror. But she turned to Chryllis nevertheless, hoping he might have a feasible plan—anything to quell the crushing anxiety that gnawed at her chest.

"Let's sneak out of here and do a flyby. See what's happening."

"We shouldn't," Jilly replied primly. But in the next instant she changed her mind. "Oh, why not?" she said. "I can't stand the suspense. Let's do it!"

***

"I'm going back!" a man cried. "I won't be run out by a few dumb animals and some pesky insects."

"Me too," another from the crowd agreed. And then a raucous noise from above drew the eyes of every human skyward. Thousands of passenger pigeons covered the sun like a thick black cloak, and in an instant, day turned to night.

A cry arose from the human tribe. This was unnatural, and they were afraid. In the meantime, the second line of the Dra offensive had taken to the sky and tilted their scales. The humans' fear turned to terror when the black sky was suddenly alight with tongues of flame.

"We're leaving!" a man exclaimed, motioning for his wife and children to follow him.

"So are we," another chimed in, racing for the overturned canoes. "We can find another place."

But the rest of the clan members huddled together, unsure of their next move. Just as the last of the passenger pigeons passed overhead, revealing the sun, waves of flying pests appeared. Once more they descended on the hapless humans, buzzing, biting, and stinging. As if that weren't enough to force the humans to retreat, the wolverine troops emerged from the forest, slinking toward the beach, fangs bared. Following them was a ferocious-looking black bear. When he emerged from the thicket, he rose to his full height, standing on his back feet and extending his claws. And behind him were the beavers, the badgers, and all the other creatures of the forest.

The humans didn't hesitate; they wanted nothing more than to leave this place as quickly as possible. They tore down to the water's edge and began pushing the canoes out into the lake. Mothers flung their children into the crude vessels and then jumped in themselves. It wasn't long before the beach was deserted. Then a victorious cry rose up from the Dras and their woodland friends.

***

Chryllis and Jilly soared above the treetops.

"Oh my goodness!" Jilly exclaimed. "Look, Chryllis! There's

Zuzu!"

Chryllis glanced down and spotted the baby Dra being led through the forest by a small girl. "That's strange," he said. "The plan was to free Zuzu, but it looks like someone's beat us to it."

"We have to do something!" Jilly exclaimed. "We must get Zuzu!"

Chryllis wasted no time. "Come on!" he cried, swooping down and navigating tree limbs like a seasoned pilot, with Jilly fast on his tail. In a matter of moments, the Dras were landing in front of a very startled Alitta and a beaming baby Zuzu.

"It's okay," Chryllis explained, raising a palm toward the girl, who stood before them quaking in fear. "We come in peace," he said.

But his words did nothing to calm the girl.

Jilly stepped forward, a welcoming smile on her face. "Hello," she said. "I'm Jilly, and this"—she gestured toward her friend—"is my best friend, Chryllis."

Alitta gazed at the two younglings in confusion. Then she turned toward Zuzu. "You know?" she asked, gesturing toward the younglings.

"Jilly, Chryllis," the baby Dra said, grinning widely. "Friends."

"Oh, friends," Alitta said. "Well then . . ."

"Thank you for caring for Zuzu," Jilly said.

"Yes," Chryllis agreed. "Many thanks."

"We'll take it from here." Jilly extended a hand toward Zuzu.

Chryllis took his cue from Jilly and grasped Zuzu's other hand. "You'd best be getting back to your own clan," he said, motioning for the girl to be on her way.

Zuzu and Alitta gazed into each other's eyes. "Bye," Alitta said, a tear rolling down her cheek.

"Bye," Zuzu replied, a sad smile on her face. "Alitta friend."

"Friend," Alitta agreed.

And then Chryllis and Jilly flapped their wings and rose up into the air with baby Zuzu between them.

"Bye," Zuzu cried. "Bye-bye, Alitta."

CHAPTER 9

ANOTHER DAY IN PARADISE

"We did it!" Madge exclaimed, eyeing the humans, who were fast retreating in their wooden vessels.

"Grrr," Gryr grumbled. "No blood."

"You cawed say that again!" Cole and his band of crows descended from the sky. "A bang-up job all around," he said.

The Dras alit as well, eager to offer their own congratulations and thanks.

"I can't believe it," Elya said, eyeing the silvery-whiskered Kahn.

"Yes," Kahn replied. "We ran them off with nary a casualty."

"My baby!" Glenis's grief-stricken wail rent the air. "Where's my girl?"

In an instant, the joyous mood vanished. The Dras and the woodland animals looked to one another shamefacedly. In all the excitement, they'd completely forgotten Zuzu.

"How could this be? Where's the child?" Ulf demanded.

At that moment, Chryllis and Jilly, with Zuzu between them, flew down and landed before Glenis. "She's right here, ma'am!" Chryllis exclaimed triumphantly.

"Safe and sound," Jilly added.

Glenis rushed toward Zuzu, sweeping the babe into her arms. "My darling girl," she said, smothering the child with kisses.

Elya sighed with relief and smiled at Ulf. "All's well that ends well," she said.

"Not quite," Jilly said, nodding toward the pathway where a confused and frightened Alitta stood trembling. "There's Zuzu's true liberator. She's the one who freed your girl."

"And now her clan has fled," Chryllis added, gesturing toward the rapidly disappearing fleet of boats. "She's all alone."

"The poor thing," Glenis murmured. "What's to be done?"

"We'll hand-deliver her!" cried a Dra teen, eager for action.

"Yes, let us do it," another piped in.

"No!" Kahn roared. "It's too risky. The girl could get hurt, and that's no way to repay her for her kindness."

"Strap her to my back," Elya said. "I'll take her."

"Are you sure about this?" Ulf asked. "It could be dangerous. I'll go instead."

"Don't be silly!" Elya turned to her mate. "You're much too big and threatening looking. You'd scare them half to death, and they're already terrified. I'll be fine."

"It's a good plan," Kahn said. "The younglings and teens can escort you."

***

"You see," Grandpa said, "Kahn was a very wise leader. He realized that the young Dras needed to feel a part of this mission of mercy. That is why he allowed the younglings the honor of flying out over the Great Lake to accompany Elya."

"I like this story, Grandpa," the boy said.

"Me too," the girl agreed.

***

When the humans saw Elya and her young escorts flying toward them, they cowered in fear. But then a woman shrieked, "They've got Alitta! My baby girl!"

Alitta pointed toward her mother, far below in a dugout canoe. Elya flew to that very spot and hovered there, all the while unstrapping the binding that secured her human passenger. Chryllis and Jilly reached for Alitta's hands and then gently lowered the girl into the dugout and her awaiting mother's arms.

"Way-ho!" the irrepressible Dra teens shouted as the transfer took place. Boisterously, they performed aeronautical stunts, rolling and diving and pumping their forearms in the air victoriously.

***

"I'm bored," Chryllis said, idly twisting a blade of grass between his long-nailed fingers.

"Me too," Jilly agreed. "After all the excitement, it seems pretty dull around here."

But then Cole plummeted down in a flurry of feathers. "Hiya, kids!" he cried. "How's tricks?"

"Hey, Cole!" Chryllis exclaimed. "Nothing much happening here these days."

"Not true, my friend," Cole replied. "The boys and me are arranging a game down by the cherry orchard. You want to play?"

"Grrr," Gryr grumbled, padding toward them. "Count me in," he said. "Anything to relieve the monotony."

"That's super," Madge said, trotting over to the small group. "It's been too long since we've had a match."

"Yeth," Toofus chimed in. "I'm getting rusthy."

Jilly raised her black brows and grinned at Chryllis. He smiled back at her and shook his head. The two clasped hands and followed Cole and his boys, Toofus and Madge, as they trudged to the cherry orchard.

"It's just another day in paradise," Jilly said.

"You can say that again," Chryllis agreed. "Can't wait to see what happens next."

***

"What does happen next, Grandpa?" the girl asked.

"Yes, Grandpa, what becomes of the Dune Dragons?" asked the boy.

"Well, that's a story for another day."

"Tell us, Grandpa," the sleepy children cried.

"Not now. It's off to bed with you, darlings."

"Good night, Grandpa."

"Good night."

THE END

CPSIA information can be obtained
at www.ICGtesting.com
Printed in the USA
LVHW111659190819
628150LV00009B/158/P